Breaking Free

Breaking Free

A JOURNEY FOR SURVIVAL

Henry Radoff

ARCHWAY
PUBLISHING

Archway Publishing books may be ordered through booksellers or by contacting:

Archway Publishing
1663 Liberty Drive
Bloomington, IN 47403
www.archwaypublishing.com
1 (888) 242-5904

Because of the dynamic nature of the Internet, any web addresses or
links contained in this book may have changed since publication and
may no longer be valid. The views expressed in this work are solely those
of the author and do not necessarily reflect the views of the publisher,
and the publisher hereby disclaims any responsibility for them.

Any people depicted in stock imagery provided by Thinkstock are models,
and such images are being used for illustrative purposes only.
Certain stock imagery © Thinkstock.

This is a work of fiction. All of the characters, names, incidents,
organizations, and dialogue in this novel are either the products
of the author's imagination or are used fictitiously.

ISBN: 978-1-4808-3914-4 (sc)
ISBN: 978-1-4808-3915-1 (e)

Library of Congress Control Number: 2016921585

Print information available on the last page.

Archway Publishing rev. date: 12/30/2016

**We Survived
Because the
Will to Live
Burns Greater
Than the Fire around Us**

DEDICATION

To my father, J. P. Radoff, who taught the Holocaust
course at Congregation Emanu El in Houston, Texas.

And

to Liny Pajgin Yollick, a survivor, who told me the basis
of the story and urged me to write this novel.

PROLOGUE

In the midst of what could be comes courage and determination. Six people survive a horrible fate by traversing a forest and becoming alpinists. Without the assistance of a prodigious guide, their journey to salvation could never have been fulfilled. This story is based upon true events.

Somewhere in the United States
Current Day

It is a gloomy, rainy day, certainly not one to go to the park and play. What to do with a seven-year-old I am babysitting. He is always restless. I promised his parents I would take him to the park, but those plans must change. After all, I am an old man, not as spirited as I used to be. But I am not so old as to have forgotten my past. My dog is as old as I am, slightly blind and arthritic, and just called *Dog*. He is always by my side. He understands that I take it slow and easy. After all, we are lucky to be alive. Heck, my grandson is lucky to be alive.

"Grandpa? Grandpa, are you awake? It is too wet go to the park. How about you tell me that story instead?"

Now that he is seven, perhaps I can tell him the whole story. "What do you say, boy?" I pat my dog. "Should I tell him the whole story?

"Get us some cookies and milk, and come sit on my lap," I respond.

When he is properly situated, I ask, "Do you want to hear the one about the people having to leave their home, cross a mountain, and go to a strange place?"

"Yes, Grandpa, that one!" replies the grandson.

"I will start the story, but if you get too frightened, you yell out and I will stop. Understood?"

"Yes, Grandpa."

CHAPTER 1

Freiburg, Germany
November 1938

Once there was a man and his wife, like your mom and dad. They lived in a house just like your home in a small, faraway town called Freiburg in Germany. It was a lively town with tree-lined streets, with alleyways covered in ivy, surrounded by a river, and on the southern edge of a big forest. In the center of the city was a town square, where on weekends a string quartet would play and the people of Freiburg would gather on blankets and have a picnic. This was such a weekend. Opposite the town square was an old synagogue. For the Jewish community, it was a gathering place where one could not only pray but also participate in many social events. Around the corner there was a major university. The man was a doctor, on the faculty of medicine at the university. He treated little boys just like you for those scrapes and cuts you little rascals get.

"Oh, Grandpa. Like the cut I have here from falling off my bicycle?" asked the grandson.

"Just like that cut."

Well, one day while the doctor was in the clinic attending to a small boy, an announcement came over the radio: "We interrupt this program for a special bulletin. Dateline: Berlin. The National Socialist Party has gained power in the Reichstag. I repeat: the National Socialist Party has gained power. Adolph Hitler is now the chancellor of Germany, our supreme leader."

"What is a supreme leader?" asked the grandson. "Is that like Superman?"

"A man, all right, but hardly super."

Now, the doctor who was treating the small boy was Jewish. He was about thirty years old, lean, and athletic-looking. Let's call him Herschel. He was married to Sophia, a beautiful, slender, soft-spoken woman in her thirties. They were originally from Holland and had settled in Freiburg so Herschel could work in the university clinic and teach at the college of medicine. They were very active in the community, participating in affairs of the synagogue and supporting the cultural programs of the city. They wanted to start a family but had been having difficulty.

"Like our family, Grandpa?"

"Just like our family."

But as hard as they tried, Sophia could not get pregnant.

Herschel examined the small boy, whose eyes were tearing. He wiped away a tear from the small boy's eyes.

"So you fell from your bicycle. Don't feel ashamed. I fell off more times than I want to remember before I could ride my bike."

"Really, Doctor?" said the boy.

"Of course. A little alcohol and a bandage, and you will be just fine."

There was a knock on the door of the examining room.

"Herr Doctor, there has been a development. Can you come out for a moment?" said the director, a rather plump and slightly balding man.

The grandfather, seeing a puzzled look on the grandson, said, "The director is like the principal in your school. He is over the teachers and when there is a problem, meets the parents. Remember when that happened to you?"

"Yes. Is the doctor going to get a spanking from the director?"

"No, this is not that kind of meeting."

After the knock, Herschel said, "Certainly, Herr Director. I am finished.

"Off you go." He helped the boy off the examining table and patted him on the rear as the boy exited. "What is it, Herr Director?"

"Come in, Herschel, and close the door. Do you know what is happening in Berlin? Today a directive came down. Under the law for reintroduction of professional service, all Jewish doctors are to be reassigned to clinics set up in a ghetto. Herschel, you have orders to go to Munich. Listen to me. Don't obey those orders. Get Sophia, and leave Germany immediately. Leave now! Go home. Pack. And Herschel, take back paths, not main roads. I hear the army is making a grand entrance into Freiburg over the town bridge, and you would not want to be on the welcoming committee. You are a fine doctor and a good man. I am going to miss you." He hugged Herschel.

"But Herr Director, are you sure? Maybe this will pass."

"I am sure. It will not pass. I have made an arrangement with an old friend, Herr Strup, to meet you at the base of the mountain outside Mullheim. He will take you to a guide who will lead you over the mountain to safety. I will monitor the conditions at Mullheim and let Herr Strup know. You might have to head south of Mullheim in the event the army is already there. Herr Strup will meet you then at that part of the mountain range north of Basel. He will provide you with a guide there to cross over the mountain. You will need to take some valuables to pay the guide."

"I have some diamonds, Herr Director, but is this all necessary?" asked Herschel.

"Yes, very necessary! Take this map of the Black Forest and the Swiss Alps. You need to cross through the Black Forest here and go to the springs outside Mullheim," he said, pointing to the map. "From there you will go to the mountain and meet Herr Strup. If the situation at Mullheim is not passable, take the alternate route I have marked through the forest to the mountain north of Basel. Either way, Herr Strup will meet you at the base of the mountain, and your guide will take you the rest of the way."

"After we cross the forest and go over the mountain, where do we go?" asked Herschel.

"To Rachel Stern's refugee camp. She set up at a ski lodge just over the mountain north of Basel. Herr Strup has already contacted her. She will issue you new Swiss passports to travel to a neutral country. Now go before it is too late. Go!" pleaded the director.

He handed Herschel the map. They shook hands and embraced. Herschel slipped out the back door, running all the way home.

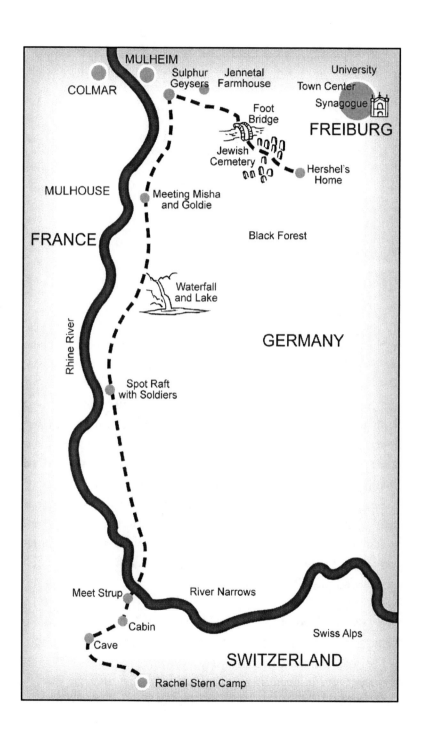

CHAPTER 2

Freiburg, Germany
November 14, 1938

At the edge of town, over the river that surrounded Freiburg, there was a small, modest cottage nestled in a garden. A window was open, allowing sunlight and a little breeze to enter, blowing the curtains and making the light dance around on the walls. Herschel and Sophia were packing. There were sounds of music coming from the direction of the town square. Sophia really didn't want to go and was taking her time. She stopped and dreamed of the good times and the friends she had in Freiburg. She also thought about her pregnancy, having just found out the day before that she was expecting. This was to be a joyous time, and she had wanted to tell Herschel the moment he came home from the clinic. She had been making a special dinner and thought they were going to celebrate. Under the circumstances, she decided to wait to tell him.

"I wouldn't want to go either, Grandpa. I would miss all my friends and school and my soccer games," said the grandson.

"They had no choice. If they stayed, bad things would happen."

"What bad things, Grandpa?"

"Be patient. You will see," Grandpa replied. "Now where was I?"

Sophia said, "Herschel, listen to that string quartet playing in the park. It seems like yesterday we were sitting in the park, picnic basket spread out on a mat surrounded by friends, peacefully bathing in the sounds of the music and—"

"Hurry, Sophia! We must go now. The soldiers are coming, and it is only a matter of time."

"I know, you don't have to repeat it. I am hurrying as fast as I can. It's just that there are so many memories," Sophia said with a sigh.

Herschel embraced her, stroked her hair, and kissed her on the cheek. "They can't take the memories. Not the memories. Now go." He gently pushed her out the door as they looked back at the cottage one last time.

CHAPTER 3

Freiburg, Germany
November 14, 1938
Kristallnacht

Outside the city, the German army moved over the mountains and through vineyards toward Freiburg, as if marching to the string quartet. Pedestrians on the street watched with stern faces as the soldiers crossed the bridge to the town center. In the park, the string quartet hurriedly finished a song and then left. Shop owners closed their shops and retreated to the backs of their stores, trying to avoid any contact with the soldiers. University students hurried along the sun-soaked, narrow streets past the Muenster Cathedral to hide in their residences. A little girl running with a prized cuckoo clock found a fountain and perched behind it, watching the soldiers entering the town square. The rabbi, with the help of his daughter Julia, ushered anyone trying to hide into the synagogue and out of the sight of the soldiers. All normal activity came to a halt.

Herschel and Sophia left their home carrying a small bag. In their haste, they had packed very little food and water. They left behind all their possessions. Herschel had collected a few diamonds for just such a day, having learned from his parents about the pogroms in Russia and how to survive. His father and mother always told him to have something of value to bargain with and that someday his life might depend on it. And now that day had come.

They walked toward a Jewish cemetery located a short distance from the cottage at the southern edge of the forest. They moved slowly, so as not to attract attention.

A dirt path led into a clearing with a small fence surrounding the graveyard. A sinister canopy of evergreens marked the beginning of the Black Forest.

"Walk slowly. Do not look suspicious. Cut through the old Jewish cemetery," Herschel whispered.

"The cemetery! Must we? Why can't we cross the bridge at town center and enter the forest that way?" replied Sophia.

"Too late. The soldiers are already in the town center. We will cross the cemetery and go over the footbridge and enter the forest. It is a longer walk but safer."

They walked through the graveyard in silence, each glancing at headstones as they went until they reached the other side of the cemetery. Just before crossing the footbridge, they heard though a loud speaker: *"Jews, come out. You won't be hurt if you come out now. Jews out now. You won't be hurt."*

Looking back toward town, they saw soldiers gathering at each corner of the square. People were rushing inside their homes to hide. They saw trucks being loaded with townspeople, their hands in the air. Soldiers with machine guns and clip boards were checking names off a list. More machine guns fired in the background as new trucks pulled up. In the distance they saw trucks unloading at the rail station. Herschel and Sophia glanced at each other in horror. Not wanting to see any more but drawn to the evolving scene, they heard more machine gun fire and earth-shaking screams. Suddenly the synagogue was enveloped in flames. They saw people rushing out into the arms of the waiting soldiers. They wondered what had happened to the rabbi and his daughter.

In the synagogue, the rabbi and his daughter, Julia, were preparing for the evening service. When they saw the soldiers crossing the bridge, they hastened congregants into the synagogue to hide. The rabbi had been the leader of his congregation for over fifty years. His daughter had grown up there after her mom died in childbirth. Julia, being somewhat of a tomboy, had climbed the mountain north of Basel on several occasions and camped out in a cave. When she saw the soldiers, she knew they must escape, climb the mountain, and hide in the cave.

"We need to leave now. I will guide you through the forest to the foot of the mountain, and we will go to that cave I camped in," Julia said. "I know a back way up the mountain through a pass that is not on any map."

The rabbi, looking disheveled and confused, replied, "You go! Save yourself! I am too old to run through a forest and climb a mountain."

Julia wouldn't take no for an answer and grabbed the hand of the rabbi and drug him toward the front of the synagogue.

As the soldiers approached the synagogue, they flung torches onto the wooden structure. Many years of decomposed wood were now ripe for burning, and the synagogue burst into flames. The rabbi and Julia were trapped. As they started toward the front of the synagogue, unknowingly into the arms of the waiting soldiers, a stout, burly figure rushed them, pulling the rabbi and Julia to the rear of the synagogue. After seeing they were safe, he spun and rushed back to the front to distract the soldiers. Julia, realizing what had happened, drug the rabbi to her secret path leading to the forest. The rabbi, relenting, allowed her to pick up the pace, and they disappeared into the darkness, on their way to the cave.

Meanwhile Herschel and Sophia, still observing the debacle, spotted a large, furry dog rushing a soldier at the front of the synagogue. The soldier in response aimed his rifle at the dog.

"Do you see that big dog attacking the soldier? He is trying to shoot the dog!" whispered Sophia.

The dog stopped suddenly and did a tight spin, causing the soldier to tumble backward, firing his rifle in the air, and then scampered off.

"Lucky for the dog the soldier fell down," whispered Sophia.

"Lucky for us the director told me what was about to happen and we left just in time!" exclaimed Herschel.

"I don't understand what's happening. I don't understand!" Sophia cried.

She sobbed uncontrollably and shook her head. Herschel grabbed her and gently placed his hand over her mouth.

He whispered, "We were just visitors in Freiburg. It was time for us to leave. Do not dwell on the past. Think of the future—our future."

Sophia, thinking of the baby, shook her head in agreement.

They realized they couldn't wait any longer. They moved hurriedly through the outer woods of the forest through pervasive darkness and hid in some dense foliage.

"Grandpa, they were lucky, and so was the dog," says the grandson.

"Yes, and it was a good thing the dog escaped!" He pats the dog on the head.

After regaining their composure, Herschel and Sophia walked through the forest, passing a small cluster of trees and heading into a nature preserve in which to take refuge for the night. According to the map, they were just outside Jennetal. Not far away they spotted lights from a half-timbered farmhouse, but they did not dare approach, for who could they trust?

"But Grandpa, where do they sleep in the forest?" asks the Grandson.

"I am getting to that part of the story. Once again, be patient," he pleads.

Herschel and Sophia gathered leaves and branches, making a bed, and ate some of the food they brought, realizing it was not enough to last until they were safe. The only sounds they heard were the continued faint sounds of gunfire and screams. They looked at each other with tears in their eyes, knowing it could have happened to them. As they rested, Sophia pondered whether this was the time to tell Herschel about the baby. She again decided to wait.

CHAPTER 4

In the Black Forest
November 14, 1938

Later that evening Herschel heard gunfire coming from the direction of the farmhouse. He stirred Sophia and told her to be quiet as he went closer to see what was happening. A German soldier was shooting at the farmhouse, and another threw torches. Suddenly the entire farmhouse was enveloped in flames.

He heard shouting from the soldiers. *"Jews, you hid Jews. This is your reward for hiding Jews."*

Herschel rushed back to Sophia and whispered what he just witnessed.

"This could have been our fate, Sophia. We need to go as far as we can from here before it gets too dark," Herschel whispered.

In silence they walked further through the damp forest floor and deeper into the woods. Sophia heard a sound coming from the brush and motioned to Herschel to be silent. In the stillness they saw a large, furry dog racing through the underbrush.

"That is the same dog that tricked the soldier, and now he is going home. Maybe we should follow him?" questioned Sophia.

"He is running too fast. We will never catch up to him,"

Herschel responded. "Besides, I have a map, and we need to follow Herr Director's instructions."

After walking a little further into the forest and through a marshy area, with dusk turning to dark, they gathered a new bed of leaves and settled down for the night. After eating, Herschel stroked Sophia's face and rubbed her temples until she fell asleep. In the distance a screech owl howled. He looked up to the treetops, feeling lucky they were still alive.

CHAPTER 5

In the Black Forest
November 15, 1938

It was dawn. Herschel and Sophia woke in each other's arms, weary of where they were. It was colder, and a light rain had fallen during the night. From the dense brush they heard faint voices of villagers observing the ruins of the farmhouse. Herschel motioned to Sophia to hastily eat a beef stick and drink some water.

"Do you have any idea where we are going, Herschel? Are we just going to hide in the forest until the soldiers go away," whispered Sophia.

"No, we are going to Mülheim. I know a place around the thermal springs and geysers where we can hide. From there it is short distance to the mountain. That is the arrangement," Herschel whispered.

"What arrangement?" asked Sophia.

"For a guide to take us over the mountains into Switzerland. The way I figure it, we can—"

"Over the mountains! Those mountains are high, cold, and slippery. What do we know about climbing a mountain? What if the

Germans are waiting for us in the mountains?" whispered Sophia in a panic.

"That is why I am made the arrangement to hire a guide. Herr Director knows this man, and he helped me make the arrangement. After we cross into Switzerland, we are going to Rachel Stern's camp." He showed her the map. "It is done, so stop worrying," whispered Herschel, caressing her face and giving her a kiss.

"I don't know, Herschel. Maybe it is safer in the forest. I'd rather die in the forest surrounded by the Lord's creatures than on some cold, snowy, desolate mountaintop," whispered Sophia.

"Would you stop! I made the arrangement. Now let's go. We must keep moving," Herschel whispered.

They spent the rest of the day carefully walking through the forest, passing medieval ruins, avoiding clearings, and staying within the safety of the heavy brush. At dusk Herschel found some wild berries to eat. He also found some rainwater collected in a hollowed-out tree. To conserve what little food and water they had, he cupped his hand and brought some of the water to Sophia to drink, and they ate the berries and rested.

"I recall when the Jews left Egypt, they ate bread fruit. This is our bread fruit!" exclaimed Herschel.

Both laughed, and after eating, they cuddled to share each other's warmth and went to sleep on another pile of branches and leaves. The forest had become their new home.

CHAPTER 6

Deeper in the Black Forest
November 16, 1938

The next morning, they woke up, brushed themselves off, ate some more berries, and started toward the springs.

They heard the sound of machine gun fire as they approached the edge of the town by the geysers. Steam was rising, forming a mist over the area, and there was a smell of sulfur in the air. There was an occasional burst of steam so dense that they could not see. It looked every inch like a Grimm's fairy-tale. After all, this was where Hansel and Gretel encountered the wicked witch. In one of these bursts, Herschel and Sophia approached the springs.

"What are the geysers, Grandpa?" asks the grandson.
"They are like a water fountain. When you turn it on, water shoots up. This is nature's water fountain," replies the grandpa, motioning with his hands.

Meanwhile, whispering and pointing to a brushy area, Herschel told Sophia to wait there.
"I am going to check out the springs."

"Herschel, don't leave me alone. I'm scared," she replied, trembling. "What if you don't come back? What if you do come back and I have been captured? Don't leave me now. Let me go to the geysers with you. Whatever happens, I want it to happen together."

Relenting, they slowly walked to the geysers and hot springs obscured by a burst of steam. Midway Herschel put his hand on Sophia's chest to stop her.

"Why did you stop? I don't see anyone. I don't hear anything. Did you?" whispered Sophia.

"No, it's a feeling. An instinct. Back into woods, now, *now!*" whispered Herschel as he pushed Sophia back toward the woods just as a German transport approached the springs.

Suddenly a soldier yelled, "*Jews come out of the forest. We know you are there. Come out now, or we will send in the dogs.*"

Herschel and Sophia froze, looking at each other, sweat pouring down their faces

"*Jews, come out,*" the soldier yelled once again.

A machine gun fired in the distance, and screams were heard. Two people emerged from the dense brush, hands raised, and the soldiers quickly seized them and placed them in the transport.

Herschel motioned to Sophia to move slowly backward until they disappeared into the safety of the forest's shadows.

"That settles it, Sophia. We must go to the mountain now. Soon the borders will be too protected and we will miss Herr Strup," whispered Herschel. Looking at the map he said, "We will go south and follow the Rhine, and from there it will be a direct path to the mountain, just as the director marked."

"But Herschel, I need to stop, to rest for a while. I am tired, and we need real food and water," whispered Sophia, thinking of their child and whether this was the right time to tell Herschel.

"I know, but it is just a matter of time before the Germans

bring dogs to search the forest. We can't be here when that happens," whispered Herschel.

"Did they bring in the dogs, Grandpa?" inquires the Grandson.

"Not yet, but they will. They always did," replies the Grandpa, sighing.

The thermal springs slowly disappeared, and the sky turned dark from the thick trees and vines as Herschel and Sophia made their way on the alternate path toward the mountain, not knowing when they would reach the mountain or whether the director told Herr Strup to meet them at the second location.

Meanwhile the director, hearing that the army had entered Mullheim, contacted Herr Strup. He hoped that Herschel had witnessed the occupation of Mullheim and followed the map south as he marked.

The rabbi and Julia traveled through the forest from another direction and avoided contact with any people, seeing only squirrels, rabbits, and birds. The rabbi reflected on how peaceful it was there and why people couldn't be like the forest animals and just get along.

CHAPTER 7

Deeper in the Black Forest
November 16, 1938

This route through the forest was rougher, and as Herschel and Sophia walked, they realized they were slowly climbing. In the distance they heard faint voices and saw shapes moving through the shadows.

"Sophia! Get down behind that bush. Do you hear the voices? Over there, voices!" whispered Herschel, pointing in the direction of the voices.

"I hear them. Do you think they are soldiers?" whispered Sophia in a panic.

"I don't know. We can't take a chance. We will wait here and watch," Herschel replied.

Out of the brush, in a clearing, appeared an older, rugged-looking man with a nose red from drinking, carrying two bags and out of breath. An older woman emerged, wearing a fur coat with an apron flapping as she went. An eight-year-old girl, looking bewildered, followed.

"So you think you know where we are. So where are we, genius?" asked the women.

"I think we are in the Black Forest," the older man replied, shrugging his shoulders.

"I know that. Where in the Black Forest?" the older women demanded.

"Somewhere by the springs—you know the thermal springs," the old man responded. "Smell the sulfur!" he said, sniffing the air and pointing up.

"You rely on your nose! You don't know nothing. Such a schlemiel. My mother warned me about marrying such a schlemiel," replied the older women.

"Not in front of the child. Save your comments for later," the older man responded.

"What is a schlemiel, Grandpa?" asks the grandson.

"Like a silly person," he responds.

"Oh, there is a kid in our school who is a schlemiel," replies the grandson.

The grandpa smiles and continues.

Herschel loudly whispered, "Psst. Over here. Psst. Over here!"

"Misha, did you make that sound?" asked the older women.

"No, Goldie," replied Misha.

"Psst. Over here, in the bushes. Come over here, quickly, quietly," Herschel whispered louder.

"Goldie, there is someone else here. Do you think it's a trap?" asked Misha. "Look over there." He pointed to where Herschel and Sophia were hiding. "Two people."

"Our people or Germans?" Goldie asked as she held out two fingers and spit on them. The little girl was whimpering.

"It's too late to turn back. We have been spotted," said Misha.

"I will hide with Sarah. You know what they will do if they find Sarah," Goldie replied.

She drug Sarah into a brushy area and waited, placing her hand over Sarah's mouth.

Misha shouted "We are lost. Just two lost people in the forest with our grandchild. We're not Jews. Just two lost *Germans* with our grandchild. We love Germany. We took a stroll with our grandchild and got—"

Herschel jumped up and grabbed him, placing his hand over his mouth, causing him to drop the bags. Sophia did the same to Goldie and Sarah.

"Quiet! I know you are Jews. We're Jews too! German soldiers are at the springs. They just arrested two people. It is just a matter of time before the dogs will be brought into the forest. We need to go—now! Deeper, away from here," whispered Herschel.

"You, you are Jews too? Hiding in the forest? You say they have dogs?" asked Goldie.

Ignoring the question, Herschel whispered, "I am Herschel, and this my wife, Sophia."

"Oh, nice to meet you. I am Misha, and that is my Goldie and Sarah, our grandchild. Sarah is eight," replied Misha proudly.

Herschel continued. "We are from Freiburg. The soldiers came in and rounded the Jews up and took them away to the train station to board trains. They destroyed the synagogue. In the forest we saw German soldiers burn a farmhouse where Jews had been hiding."

"They did this. What can we do? Where can we go? I mean Goldie and I, we are just poor Jews. The Germans came into our village too, and we fled like the others. Sarah got separated from our son, so we took her with us. We only had time to take some food and schnapps." He pointed to the bags. "Been wandering in this forest for days," replied Misha.

"You say you are going to where?" asked Goldie. "In the forest, just hiding in the forest till the food runs out and we starve to death? What about Sarah? How can she last?" exclaimed Goldie.

"Not hiding in the forest. Using the forest to get to the mountain to cross over to Switzerland," Herschel proclaimed.

"We cross a mountain? We're not mountain climbers!" exclaimed Goldie.

Sophia replied, "Herschel has made an arrangement." She showed her the map. "He has hired a guide to take us over the mountain. And you can come too. It is the only way you will survive. You can't stay in the forest. The soldiers will track you down. Now come with us!"

"What do you think, Goldie? Should we go with them?" asked Misha.

Goldie regained her composure and wiped her eyes with her apron.

"Do we have a choice? It is Sarah's"—she looked at the child—"only hope. Let's go. Besides, it's an adventure, more excitement than I have had in many years living with you!" replied Goldie.

The grandson laughs. "They are funny, aren't they, Grandpa? And Sarah is scared, right, Grandpa?"
Grandpa nods his head in agreement and continues.

They made their way back into the forest, traversing thicker foliage and sharper terrain. Their footing was uneven, and they were starting to climb. This part of the forest was at a higher elevation. They came across a waterfall and small pond in a clearing. Observing whether it was safe to enter the clearing, Herschel decided to take a chance, and they walked over to the waterfall. On any other occasion this would be a perfect holiday campsite. They gathered the water from the falls to wash their faces and drink. Goldie took out the food and the schnapps, and they are sparingly and sipped the schnapps. The sun was setting, and the darkness was surrounding what little light remained. They decided to stay there for the night. It was turning colder, and a mist appeared through the trees. They found a clump of brush and made a bed, falling asleep to the sounds of the waterfall.

CHAPTER 8

At the waterfall in the Black Forest
November 17, 1938

Dawn entered, with glistening sunlight reflecting off the waterfall. Even the dense foliage couldn't keep out the sunlight. The cold had become a factor, as well as the elevation. Breathing had become more difficult. Having made a small fire so as not to draw attention, Goldie decided she was going to cook. She opened one of the bags they brought and took out eggs and bread. Out of the other bag she took a small pan. She started cooking the eggs and bread together. Misha took out the schnapps and a bottle of water and took a sip of both. He gave Sarah a drink of the water and stroked her face.

"Some vacation, right, Sarah?" said Misha.

Herschel woke up, rubbed his eyes, and saw Goldie cooking. He ran over to her.

"Goldie, put out that fire. The smoke will draw attention!" Herschel yelled.

Goldie responded, "I will after the egg bread is cooked."

"As much as I would like some cooked food, we can't risk it," Herschel replied as he grabbed the pan and threw dirt on the fire.

Having smothered it, he scattered the embers. Misha grabbed

some of the egg bread out of the pan and stuffed it into his mouth and gave some to Sarah. Sophia woke, rubbed her eyes, and brushed her hair back. Leaving the pan, Herschel took some of the egg bread to Sophia. He kissed her and told her to enjoy the last of the cooked food. There would be no more fires in the open.

Goldie took the pan to the waterfall to clean. This looked as good as any place to dump the scraps from the pan and wash it, thought Goldie. As Goldie reached for a tree limb to brush away the scraps, an arm came out of the brush and grabbed Goldie, covering her mouth as she was about to scream.

A man appearing about thirty, rugged-looking, hunter type, wearing a lightweight fur coat, wool hat, and boots hovered over Goldie, still covering her mouth and looked toward the clearing.

"Surely you are a Jew. They pay good for Jews! You come with me to Mullheim!" commanded the man.

The huntsman covered her with part of a cape made out of a parachute as Goldie tried to resist.

"He is a bad guy, right, Grandpa?" asks the grandson.

"He is. But wait to hear what happens," the grandpa replies.

Placing the grandson down from his lap and patting the dog, he continues.

CHAPTER 9

At the Waterfall in the Black Forest
November 17, 1938

Herschel, looking for a branch to use to cover their tracks, heard a disturbance. He went back to Misha.

"Misha. I heard a strange sound coming from the waterfall," whispered Herschel. "Sophia, stay here with Sarah." He motioned to Sophia to wait in the brush. "Misha, come with me, quietly." Misha nodded his head.

They made their way toward the waterfall when Herschel saw the huntsman's back, his hand over Goldie's mouth. He motioned to Misha.

"You will distract him, and I will come from the rear and knock him out."

Misha walked into the clearing and toward the huntsman. The huntsman, seeing Misha and figuring that two Jews paid better than one, drug Goldie toward Misha when Herschel, approaching from the rear, grabbed the huntsman's neck. The huntsman dropped to the ground, releasing Goldie. He lay there motionless.

"Herschel, you killed him. Just like that." He snapped his finger.

"He is dead. How did you do that?" Misha exclaimed, having felt the huntsman for a pulse.

"Easy. Just apply pressure here." He looked like he was reaching for Misha, and Misha reacting by pulling back.

"No, I take your word for it. But how did—"

"I know? Because I am a doctor. Now please"—he gestured with his hands—"can we go?" Herschel responded.

Herschel drug the body of the huntsman into the thick brush. He took the parachute cape, coat, and hat. He covered the body with tree limbs and used a branch to erase his footprints.

"He will be found when they bring in the dogs," Herschel whispered.

Herschel handed the coat to Goldie to put on and placed the parachute cape and the hat into one of the bags Misha was carrying.

"Not only do we need to watch for soldiers but for huntsmen too," Herschel whispered.

"Thank you, Misha," she said, giving him a hug. "I take back saying you are a schlemiel," Goldie whispered. "And thank you, Doctor Herschel." She gave him a hug as well.

"I told you we are all in this together," Herschel replied.

They joined up with Sophia and Sarah. Herschel took the parachute cape out of the bag and wrapped it around Sophia, who was shivering, and told her what happened. They gathered their belongings and left the campsite. Sophia, having cuddled Sarah, wondered when she should tell Herschel about their baby and again decided to wait.

CHAPTER 10

Rhine River South
November 18, 1938

In the morning they climbed a small rise and through the thick foliage saw a river gently flowing at the perimeter of the forest.

"The Rhine," exclaimed Herschel.

As they watched, a barge descended slowly, floating on the Rhine bearing soldiers. The chatter of the soldiers filtered through the forest.

After the barge safely passed, Herschel motioned for them to walk in the direction the Rhine was flowing, staying safely secluded in the forest.

Another barge followed, this time carrying arms and supplies.

"The soldiers' base must be where the Rhine meets the mountain and turns," Herschel whispered, looking at the map. "We will walk in that direction but stay hidden in the forest. When we get to the edge of the forest, we will wait until it is clear and find Herr Strup."

"But how will we cross the river?" Misha asked.

"We will find a way when we get there. Now go!" exclaimed Herschel.

As they slowly walked, another barge came down the Rhine

bearing soldiers. Herschel motioned for them to move back into thicker brush, but before he could join them, a soldier on the barge spotted the movement in the brush and saw Herschel. He raised his rifle to shoot, but just as he was about to fire, the barge took a turn, throwing him against the side of the railing. Herschel, seeing the soldier pointing the rifle, rushed into the thicker brush, joining the rest, whispering to be quiet and not to make any movements. The soldier, regaining his balance but having lost sight of Herschel and the barge moving faster down the river, gave up the hunt and joined the others, electing not to say anything for fear he would get in trouble for not having fired his rifle.

"That was a close," said Herschel. "We must stay away from the river."

They continued to walk in the deeper fringes of the forest until dusk and find a secluded spot to make camp.

"Tomorrow we will reach the base of the mountain and look for Herr Strup," said Herschel.

CHAPTER 11

South in the Black Forest
November 19, 1938

The climb was more severe now that they had come closer to the perimeter of the forest. The thick, bushy growth of vegetation was thinning and the air was colder. The terrain was less marshy and more jagged. Sarah was being carried by Misha, and Herschel was helping Sophia, who was experiencing some discomfort from the pregnancy. After resting, they commenced their journey, approaching the forest edge. They saw German soldiers with machine guns drawn on patrol, one on their side of the Rhine and the other at the base of the mountain. As they peered through some dense foliage, they watched the German border guards meticulously work their way up and down. In the distance they saw the snow white mountains and frosted slopes.

Looking up at the mountains, Sophia whispered, "Herschel, they are beautiful. Goldie, Misha, come look! The mountains are glowing, and when we climb over them, we will be free."

"If we get there," said Goldie, pausing to look at Sarah.

"Look at those soldiers. They won't let us pass. How are we going to get around them Herschel?" asked Goldie.

"And how are we going to cross the river?"

"Keep your voices down. Don't worry about the soldiers. They will have to return to their camp eventually. So we wait. Meanwhile that soldier," Herschel said, pointing to the one on their side of the Rhine, "will join the other. He has to cross the river so we watch him to see how he does. We just stay here and observe as long as it takes until they move on."

"But when?" asked Sophia.

"They will move on when they think no one is here and they are supposed to report to their post," responded Herschel.

"What if they come back this way?" asked Misha.

"Then we go back into the forest. That is why one of us will always be watching. Now, no more talking. Be patient," Herschel replied.

They positioned themselves in the thick brush. Herschel timed the soldiers pacing along the base of the mountain and figured they would soon have to move on. The Black Forest was enormous and ended at the turn of the Rhine River. He figured that the soldiers' post was there.

Sarah and Goldie were together, and Goldie distracted Sarah by quietly playing a game.

"Sarah, let's see if you can guess what I have in my right hand," whispered Goldie.

"Let me see. I think you have a flower in your right hand," Sarah whispered in reply.

"Why do you think I have a flower?" asked Goldie.

"Because you like flowers and are always picking them!" whispered Sarah.

"That's a good answer, Sarah," Goldie said, hugging her. "Now let's see what is in my hand." Goldie opened her hand to reveal a candy that she had placed in her apron, which Sarah took and ate.

Meanwhile the soldiers lingered at the border for some time and finally started to gather their belongings. It wouldn't be long before they reported to their post.

"Herschel, how are we really going to climb this mountain?" Misha whispered, pointing to the jagged edges and snowy peaks.

"Misha, when we find our guide, we *will* climb this mountain!" Herschel responded. "For now we wait. I only count two soldiers, and it looks like they are preparing to leave."

The soldier on their side of the Rhine walked toward the forest where they were hiding, stopped, and lit a cigarette. He took a puff and blew smoke in their direction. He began to observe the foliage and yelled back to the other soldier that he was going to check the perimeter of the forest.

Herschel, seeing this, motioned for the rest to move back quickly.

Just as the soldier approached where they were hiding, the other soldier yelled, "Come back, we will be late to report, and you know what that means."

"Yeah, yeah," replied the soldier. He took a cursory glance and rushed back, crossing a footbridge the Germans had built over the narrowest part of the river.

Once again fate was on their side.

Herschel, watching the soldiers, knew now how they would cross the Rhine.

CHAPTER 12

Somewhere in the United States
Current day

The grandson, having climbed up on his grandpa's lap once again and holding a blanket to his face, sleepily looks up.

"Are you getting tired? Perhaps I should stop so you can go to bed. We can finish tomorrow," says the grandpa.

The grandson sits up to show that he was not sleepy. "Please, Grandpa, don't stop. I want to hear the rest tonight."

The grandpa brushes back the grandson's hair from his face and continues.

"Remember the guide that is taking them over the mountain? Well, he has a dog. Not just any dog but a Leonberger."

"A Leonberger?" asks the grandson. "What kind of dog is that?"

"Well, since you ask, over a hundred years ago the mayor of a little German city called Leonberg wanted to do something for his city that would always be remembered. He decided that as one of his mayoral duties, he would breed a dog as a tribute to his city. So he bred a Newfie and Saint Bernard with a Great Pyrenees. The result was a dog with lion-like looks and a deep bark, something like our dog." He patted the dog on the head. "This dog, he thought, would put his city on the map. So that is how the Leonberger came about and became the symbol of the city."

"Like on a stamp?" asks the grandson.

"Something like that," replies the grandpa, smiling.

"The Leonberger became one of the most useful dogs in the mountains of Germany and Switzerland, finding downed skiers and lost mountain climbers. Herr Strup had just such a dog. He was proud of his dog. After all, he was a direct descendent of the first Leonberger. He had trained him to be a tracker and to assist him in his glory days of climbing the Alps. On more than one occasion, his Leonberger had rescued him from a bad decision, a wrong turn, or a dangerous ledge. He was like the son he never had."

"Where are they going after they climb the mountain?" asks the grandson.

"Remember, they hope to find the Stern base camp, just on the other side of the mountain."

"Stern base camp—what is that, Grandpa?" inquires the grandson.

"It is a big camp with tents set up and armed personnel on the perimeters," he says, motioning with his hands. "Rachel Stern converted a ski lodge to a rescue camp and welcomed all who escaped."

"She is a good person, right, Grandpa?"

"Very good person. She saved many lives."

"Grandpa. What about Herschel and ...?" asks the grandson.

"Be patient. They are still in the forest," replies the Grandpa.

CHAPTER 13

Base of the Mountain
November 19, 1938

Herschel looked toward the clearing through the trees. The soldiers were finally gone. Now was the time to go to the base of the mountain and look for Herr Strup.

"Time to go. Come on!" Herschel whispered to Sophia, motioning the rest to join them.

Misha and Goldie had fallen asleep. Sarah was sleeping in Goldie's lap. Sophia shook Goldie and Misha and quietly whispered, "Herschel says it's clear. We must go now before it gets too dark. Do you want me to carry Sarah?"

"Just give me moment," Misha replied. He rubbed his eyes, bent over, and picked up the sleeping Sarah from Goldie's lap.

"I will carry Sarah," Misha replied. Goldie followed Sophia with Misha at the rear.

Herschel was already in the open and moving toward the base of the mountain. He crossed the footbridge and searched for the guide.

"Come on, we are going to lose Herschel. And then what are we going to do? This is his guide, not ours," Goldie whispered.

Sophia and Goldie ran out of the forest to catch up to Herschel, who was already at the mountain base searching for Herr Strup. Misha followed, carrying Sarah.

Herr Strup, a rugged mountaineer type, always lived on the mountain, having no use for the city or city life. He would venture into town for supplies and an occasional doctor's appointment, but for the most part the mountain was his life and his dog his family. He saw Herschel and called over his dog.

"Here Prinz. Here boy. That's a good dog," he said, patting him and giving him a treat. "See over there," he said, pointing in the direction of Herschel." That's Herr Director's friend. Go, Prinz. Greet him," Herr Strup commanded.

Prinz ran over to Herschel. Sarah woke up. She was disoriented and started crying.

Sophia, seeing the dog approaching Herschel, became worried.

"Herschel, look out. The border guards' dog is coming toward you!" yelled Sophia.

Sophia wildly motioned to Misha and Goldie to stop as Herschel yelled at them to go back into the forest. Goldie in retreating ran into Misha, who stumbled but held on to Sarah.

"We are all going to be found and killed. Killed! You hear me, Misha. Hurry, hide Sarah!" cried Goldie.

"I hear you, Goldie. But what about Herschel?" asked Misha.

"He would want it this way," yelled Sophia. "Oh God! Run."

Prinz jumped on Herschel and started licking his face.

"A friendly border dog? Who do you belong to? Certainly not the Germans!" exclaimed Herschel.

Herr Strup, seeing that Herschel and Prinz had met, ran to them.

"Are you Herr Strup?" asked Herschel.

"I am," replied Herr Strup.

"My name is Herschel. My wife Sophia and two other friends and their grandchild are hiding in the forest."

"Good. You have met Prinz, my dog. It is safe. Call them out. I just passed the soldiers going in the other direction. It will be some time before any come back," replied Herr Strup.

"Sophia, Misha, Goldie, it's safe. Come meet our guide, Herr Strup. Cross the footbridge," Herschel yelled, pointing to the bridge.

"Oh, I'm not your guide," responded Herr Strup.

"I don't understand. Herr Director said he arranged with you to be our guide," questioned Herschel.

"He arranged for a guide. Your guide will be here. Wait until the others gather, and I will tell you everything."

Sophia crossed the footbridge and joined Herschel. "Thank God you're all right." She hugged Herschel. "When I saw that dog coming at you ..." said Sophia, worried.

"It's okay. It's Herr Strup's dog. Herr Strup, this is my wife, Sophia, and our new friends, Misha, Goldie, and Sarah."

"Nice to meet all of you. Especially you, Sarah. Prinz loves children! You can pet him if you want," exclaimed Herr Strup.

The dog jumped up on Misha to lick Sarah, who reached down to pet him.

"Herschel, is this like the dog we saw in Freiburg and again in the forest?" whispered Sophia, pointing to Prinz.

Herschel, examining Prinz more closely, whispered in response, "It might be."

"Now follow me to my cabin," said Herr Strup. "It is just a short walk up the mountain. And don't be afraid. The mountain looks ferocious, but it is really, how you say, a pussy cat!" exclaimed Herr Strup.

They all laughed and walked off with Herr Strup, Prinz leading the way.

"Would you have been afraid of the dog?" asks the grandpa.

"Yes, but if it was our dog," the grandson said, petting the dog, "I would not be afraid. What happens next, Grandpa?"

"Well, let's see, where did I leave off? At the cabin on the mountain. Oh yes."

The cabin was just a few yards up the side of the mountain, totally covered by brush so it could not be seen from the base of the mountain. Inside Herr Strup placed wood in the fireplace and made a fire. Herschel, Sophia, Misha, Sarah, and Goldie, shivering from the cold, warmed themselves. Sarah went over to Prinz and quietly played with him.

"Who is hungry?" asked Herr Strup. "I thought so. On the stove I am cooking a liver dumpling soup and—"

"My favorite," said Sophia. "And I thought I would never have liver dumpling soup again."

"So, Herr Strup, when do we meet our guide?" asked Herschel.

"In due time," he responded.

Herschel reached into his pocket. "Here are some diamonds Herr Director promised. I want you to give them to the guide when he comes."

"Just hold on to them. I will take them after you have been trained and you have met your guide," Herr Strup responded.

"Trained? What do you mean, trained?"

"What do you think it means? Trained. Have you crossed a snowy mountain before?" asked Herr Strup.

"None of us have. You are right. We do need training. So we wait for the guide to train us?" asked Herschel.

"No. I will train you. But for now just eat and get a good night's rest. I am sorry that I don't have beds for all of you, but I do have sleeping blankets for the floor and a comforter for Sarah."

"Seeing as we have been sleeping on leaves, the floor and blankets sound great!" exclaimed Sophia.

"You can wash up over here. After eating I will roll out the sleeping blankets," replied Herr Strup.

They all washed up and enjoyed their first real meal in several days since hiking in the forest. Afterward they prepared for bed.

Sarah said her prayers. "I lay me down to sleep, so bless Nana Goldie and Grandpa Misha and Herschel and Sophia and Prinz and Herr Strup. Amen. Amen."

Sarah cuddled in her comforter between Goldie and Misha. Herschel and Sophia cuddled in their blankets. Prinz lay at Sarah's feet, and Herr Strup (after pausing to look at them and smiling) turned out the light and went into the other room.

CHAPTER 14

Herr Strup's Cabin
November 20, 1938

Sunlight came into the cabin through the trees. A light snow had fallen during the night. Herschel was the first up.

"Get up, you sleepyheads. We have some learning to do. Herr Strup is going to show us how to climb the mountain, and he needs everyone's attention," said Herschel.

The group slowly rose, washed, and sat on the floor by the fire. Herr Strup brought them coffee and rolls and warm milk for Sarah. He rolled out a map and pointed to it.

"On this map is shown the nasty ridges and bad rock, which you are to avoid. Also the mountain passes you will travel through to avoid having to climb steep peaks. You will walk though valleys as well," he said, pointing to the map. "Your guide knows every inch of this mountain, so you must follow whatever he does."

Herr Strup brought out some snow shoes and a smaller pair for Sarah, some snow walker picks, carabiners, S-Biners, ropes, and a small shovel blade.

"Put these on to get a feel of them. We are going out into the snow so you can practice your footing. The picks, carabiners,

S-Biners, and rope will be used in your climbing and descending. The shovel will be useful in preparing the camp site. For now just practice walking around. You all will be alpinists!" Herr Strup exclaimed.

He opened the cabin door. A rush of cold air came in, and everyone shuddered.

"Better get used to the cold because you all are going to be cold for some time. But it is a good cold. It will save your life."

They all went outdoors, where they were met by Prinz.

"The first thing I want you to do is to walk around in the snow, to break in your shoes," said Herr Strup. "While you are walking, observe the ground. Look for rocks jutting out of the snow. And watch Prinz as he knows the terrain, and he will avoid those pesky hidden granite rocks. Sarah, try to walk on your own."

He handed Herschel the rope.

"After walking around, tie yourselves together by fastening the rope with the carabiners," he said, showing them how to do so. "Use the shovel blade to remove small rocks in your path. Use the ice pick to cut ice steps where needed and to pull yourself up a steep incline by jamming it behind a large rock. Here, let me demonstrate." He showed them how to use the pick. "Most of your crossing will be through passes at relatively low attitude and between peaks, but just in case you encounter rougher terrain, you need the ice pick and shovel."

"What about a compass?" Herschel asked.

"You won't need a compass. Your guide knows the right direction. You just need to worry about your footing and following your guide," responded Herr Strup.

He handed Herschel several small flasks and backpacks loaded with nonperishable food and water.

"Almost as important is what is in these flasks. It's schnapps. Each of you should sip during your climb. The schnapps will keep you warm, and in the event you fall and open a wound, you can pour some of the schnapps to cleanse the wound," Herr Strup further directed. "Of course the backpacks have your supplies, and if I have figured correctly, there is more than enough to last until you get to the camp."

He handed several small thermoses to Herschel.

Herr Strup continued. "In these is sugared water. The sugar should keep the water from freezing, but I would keep it close to your body just in case. It is very important to keep hydrated. Even when you don't feel thirsty, drink a little. Make sure Sarah drinks."

"What about a first-aid kit?" asked Herschel.

"Sorry, I lost my first-aid kid on my last climb and never got around to replacing it," replied Herr Strup. "It is better that you have the schnapps to pour on the wound. Besides, you're a doctor; use your skills.

"Now let's do some climbing. Put on the packs. Here, Prinz," he said, calling the dog over. "Herr Doctor, you and your party follow Prinz up that small peak." He pointed to a small rise through the trees. "You do what Prinz does. If he stops, you stop. If he lays on the ground, you lay on the ground. And no talking. You give hand signals to each other. Practice using the pick and tying yourself together with the ropes."

"What kind of hand signals?" said Herschel.

"You work it out among yourselves. Now go while it is still light," replied Herr Strup.

They set out following Prinz to climb their first rise. The terrain was rough and covered with snow. Prinz made his way up the slope, with the rest following from behind. The packs were heavy, but knowing their value, each carried them without complaining. Sarah managed to walk for a while but had to be carried most of the way, adding weight to the backpack. Prinz led them down, and they climbed again using the rope and pick. After a while they rested and drank some of the water and sipped the schnapps. Prinz led them up and down several more times.

"Just look at that dog. He climbs like there is no mountain!" exclaimed Goldie.

"Quiet. Remember what Herr Strup said, no talking, only hand signals," cautioned Herschel.

Goldie put up her hands and began motioning wildly.

"Goldie, what are you saying?" asked Misha, mimicking her hand signals while Sarah laughed.

"Both of you quiet. Watch me. If my finger is pointed in a direction, that means go in that direction. If my palm is up, it means stop. If my hand is palm down, it means lay down," replied Herschel.

Prinz took them next on a route between some thick foliage and large rocks to the top of a small peak, which they reached in late afternoon. After resting and drinking, they made their way down to the cabin to be greeted by Herr Strup. Their first adventure on the mountain had been exhausting, and Herschel wondered if they could really succeed.

CHAPTER 15

At the Mountain Base
November 20, 1938

The solitary lookout at the base of the mountain was joined by a commandant and his regiment.

"Any Jews try to cross the border?" asked the commandant, a large, slender man with steely blue eyes and a fierce determination to complete whatever was assigned to him. He would kill rather than take hostages. Because of his undying determination, he had risen quickly in the local party ranks.

"No Jews. Nobody but an old man and his dog," replied the soldier. "He was walking with his dog, you know just strolling on the mountain."

"And where did this old man and dog go?" asked the commandant, becoming impatient.

"Up the mountain, Herr Commandant."

"And why didn't you detain him for questioning?" yelled the commandant.

"Questioning? About what, Herr Commandant?"

The commandant slapped him on the side of the face with a glove. "About what he was doing on the mountain, you fool."

Puzzled, the soldier responded, "He was an old man just walking his dog. He wouldn't know anything."

Frustrated, the commandant addressed the entire regiment. "An old man with a dog was seen yesterday going up the mountain. Tomorrow we will go up the mountain and find this old man. That understood?"

"Yes, Herr Commandant."

"Tonight we will make camp here. Prepare the climbing gear for tomorrow. And you," he said, pointing to the border soldier, "will lead the way."

CHAPTER 16

At Strup's Cabin
November 21, 1938

The next day they practiced once more, Prinz leading the way.

"Going down is easier than going up," exclaimed Misha.

"Yes, but you still must be careful of your footing," said Herschel.

"My footing is excellent. I could get used to climbing," replied Misha.

"You will be very used to climbing by the time we get to the other side of the mountain!" exclaimed Herschel.

"It is so beautiful here," Sophia said with a sigh. "The snow on the tree limbs and the rocks—the sun setting on the peaks."

After they finished, Prinz led them back down to the cabin, and they were greeted by Herr Strup. It was dusk, and they were tired and hungry.

"Here, Prinz. Good boy," he said, handing him a bone. "For the rest of you, come in and warm yourselves. Soup is ready. You need to sleep so you can get an early start. The soldiers will be out on the mountain early, and we need to move fast."

"What about the guide. Don't we want to wait for him?"

"Don't worry. The guide will be here," Herr Strup responded.

Herr Strup rolled out the sleeping bags and placed them by the fire. Herschel and Sophia snuggled in their sleeping bags. Misha and Goldie struggled with getting into their bags. Sarah slipped into her comforter, and Prinz positioned himself at her feet, chewing on a bone.

"Try to sleep. Tomorrow our guide will take us up the mountain," said Herschel.

Misha exclaimed, "Like Moses went up Mount Sinai! Like Moses!"

"Yes, like Moses," Goldie said with a sigh.

CHAPTER 17

Herr Strup's Cabin
November 22, 1938

The mountain was dark, and the only light came from some burning embers in the fireplace. Herr Strup was already up, busily making coffee and warming some pastries and milk. Herschel stirred, but Sophia, Goldie, Sarah, and Misha were still sleeping.

"Herschel, come over here. I want to tell you before the rest are awake," whispered Herr Strup.

Herschel quietly, without disturbing the others, slipped out of the blanket and tiptoed toward Herr Strup. Prinz was still chewing on the bone that was his reward from the night before.

"Herschel, your guide has been with you since we met!" exclaimed Herr Strup.

"So you are the guide?" asked Herschel.

"No, Prinz is your guide."

"Prinz!" said Herschel as he backed away in disbelief. He said Prinz's name so loud the dog dropped the bone and came to him.

"Prinz! A dog! Prinz! Herr Strup, I can see that Prinz is very smart, very loyal and resourceful, but you are asking us to put our lives in the hands of a dog," pled Herschel.

"I understand, Herschel. But this is no ordinary dog. I have crossed these mountains into Switzerland with Prinz many times. There is no better guide. He hears and sees before any human can hear or see. He is a master of identifying the usual. If you follow him, all of you will be safe," Herr Strup responded. "A couple of days ago he outwitted a German soldier firing on him. I trust him with my life, and so can you."

"So this is the dog that tripped the soldier and escaped! I don't know. I mean, how do I explain this to the others, to Sophia, my wife? They are expecting a human guide. Can't you come with us? Can the dog be the guide but to the others it can appear that you are the guide?" asked Herschel.

"No. I am too old and would just slow you down. With Sarah it will be slow enough. When I climb with Prinz, we take our time. If we encountered a soldier like we did a couple of days ago, he would just see an old man and his dog on the mountain. But with you it would be different. Questions would be asked, and more than likely there would be an arrest or worse. No, you cannot afford to be slowed down. I will help you explain to the others," replied Herr Strup.

"Here are the diamonds," replied Herschel, handing them to Herr Strup.

"Keep them. You will need them to bargain with in the event you are caught and when you reach freedom to go wherever it is safe. See this collar," he said, handing the collar to Herschel.

"Yes. It's a dog's collar," replied Herschel.

"That's right. It has a secret compartment on the reverse side," he said, turning it over to show Herschel. "Put the diamonds in the collar and put the collar on Prinz. Now, come, wake the others. They must be told now that Prinz is the guide, and you must leave at once."

He started clapping his hands in order to wake the others.

"Come on, you sleepyheads. Wake up. You need to get an early start."

"Is the guide here? Are we ready to go?" asked Sophia.

"Where is he? I want to meet him. I want to tell him to take it easy on me. I am an old women and with Sarah ..." Goldie pled.

"I am afraid you will have to tell him in dog language," replied Herschel.

"Dog language. What do you mean?" asked Goldie.

"I mean Prinz is our guide," Herschel replied.

There was a long pause in the room. Sophia, Misha, and Goldie looked at Prinz, and Prinz barked.

"Prinz. Our guide! This can't be true. I mean, Herr Strup is the guide. You are making a joke." Misha laughed. "That was good, Herschel," said Misha, patting him on the back.

"No, it is true. Herr Strup is too old to guide us. Prinz knows the mountain. We must trust his judgment. We have no other choice. We can't go back," replied Herschel.

Herr Strup reassured them. After a reflective pause, they resolved to follow Prinz. After all, they were alpinists now. They ate a last meal with Herr Strup and then assembled outside. With backpacks in place and all the climbing gear, Prinz commenced to lead them away from the cabin. They looked back at Herr Strup and waved, and he waved back. He watched them until they were out of sight and then retreated into the cabin. There was a cool breeze and no sound. After a while, they stopped to rest. So far, so good. It was slow going, but Prinz knew the direction. Goldie and Sophia tried to keep warm, pulling their coat sleeves down to cover their hands. Sarah was wrapped in the parachute and being carried by Misha. They continued until dusk. Prinz stopped before reaching a small clearing, and they made camp for the night.

"It's cold, Misha. Come warm me," Goldie pleaded.

Misha went over to Goldie and rubbed her hands and her feet until she was warm and did the same to Sarah.

"Would you believe just a few days ago we were in our home, cooking diner, saying the Sabbath prayers, listening to music from the town square?" said Sophia.

"Just a few days ago, Goldie and I were doing the same," replied Misha. "And now on this mountain side, who would believe!" exclaimed Goldie.

In the distance they heard shouting and machine gun fire. The sounds echoed through the mountain. Prinz moved into some brush close by, and they followed.

"Soldiers?" asked Misha.

"Yes," whispered Herschel.

"How close?" asked Misha.

"It is hard to tell. Prinz isn't moving, so we should just stay here until he thinks it's safe to go," replied Herschel. Goldie held Sarah and motioned to her not to speak.

"I don't think it will ever be safe," Sophia said, sighing.

"It only needs to be safe enough to escape," replied Herschel.

They waited for a short while, and then Prinz moved back to the camp site he had chosen, and they followed. Herschel took out some dried beef sticks and crackers, and they passed it among themselves and ate slowly and quietly. A flask of warm schnapps was passed between them and the thermos of sugar water for Sarah. They each took a sleeping bag, and Sarah was rolled into the blanket with the parachute still around her. Goldie sang quietly to Sarah, rocking her back and forth in her arms as she closed her eyes. It was peaceful now and deceptively quiet.

"What about Herr Strup, Grandpa?"

"I am coming to that part of the story."

CHAPTER 18

Herr Strup's Cabin
November 22, 1938

Back at the cabin, Herr Strup was startled by loud knocks on his door.

"Who's there? Speak up! Who is it?" asked Herr Strup, thinking Prinz might have led them back to the cabin.

He waited by the door and listened, but there was no response.

Suddenly the door was forced open, and the commandant yelled, "Where are the *Jews* you are hiding? You can't fool us."

"What Jews?" asked Herr Strup. "No Jews here, see! Look around the cabin. I told you I am alone."

"Shut up, old man," yelled the commandant as he slapped Herr Strup so hard he fell back against the fireplace. Blood seeped from the back of his head as he tried to stand.

"No one here but the old man? Search for the others. And where is his dog?" yelled the commandant.

"Speak up, old man." He shook Herr Strup. "Where is that dog of yours?"

"Gone. Left earlier to go down the mountain. He will be back," cried Herr Strup.

"I don't believe you. Tell us who else was here and where that dog really is," yelled the commandant, striking Herr Strup once more so hard blood seeped from his nose and his mouth. He fell back again, hitting the fireplace hard, and slipped lifeless onto the floor of the cabin.

One of the soldiers rushed over and took his pulse and shook his head.

"Leave him. We will wait here until dawn. When the dog returns, it will take us to the others," replied the commandant coldly.

CHAPTER 19

On the Mountain
November 23, 1938

The sun rose, and the day looked good for climbing. Prinz was already walking the perimeter as Herschel woke the others. Sophia gathered the sleeping bags and rolled them up.

Herschel told Misha, "Find a large branch so we can sweep the area. We can't leave any tracks in the event we are followed."

"Okay, Herr Commandant," Misha replied.

While Misha was sweeping the area, Goldie took out the rations and gave everyone some dried fruit and a beef stick and a drink. They slowly ascended the mountain, faithfully following Prinz through a pass. Herschel noticed some footprints in the snow on the other side of the pass. He bent over and examined them.

"These are fresh. Must have been the sounds we heard last night!" exclaimed Herschel. "Since the prints were facing downward, they were descending the mountain."

"Are they soldiers?" asked Misha.

"Prinz knows. He is still climbing. If they are soldiers' prints, he will stop us, and we will hide," Herschel replied.

"You put a lot of faith in that dog," Misha responded.

"I have seen him react to the soldiers before, so I trust his instinct," replied Herschel.

They continued to ascend, stopping only briefly to catch their breath.

"Look how beautiful the mountain is. And look how far we have come. I can almost see the top," exclaimed Sophia.

"But when we get to the top, do we know what is on the other side?" questioned Goldie.

"No, but what difference does it make? If we don't go to the other side, we will not make it to freedom!" exclaimed Herschel.

"Freedom! I like the sound of the word," yelled Misha.

Suddenly Prinz stopped in his tracks. The others followed. Prinz lay down in the snow. The others moved back into some heavy brush and did likewise. There was no sound. There was no movement. Prinz waited, as did the others. Two soldiers appeared on patrol. They spotted Prinz.

"Here, boy. What are you doing so far up the mountain?" one of the soldiers shouted. He took down his gun and pointed it at Prinz.

"How about some practice?" said one of the soldiers.

"Let me shoot him. It was your turn last time," said the other.

"That was a rabbit, and it was too easy," responded the first soldier.

While the two soldiers argued, Prinz bolted forward and attacked the first soldier, biting him on the leg, causing the rifle to discharge, impacting the second soldier.

"Idiot! You shot me," yelled the soldier.

Prinz ran in the opposite direction down the mountain. The wounded soldier took down his rifle and pointed it at the first soldier. The first soldier shoved it aside.

"I didn't shoot you, the dog did. Let's get him," replied the other soldier.

Both soldiers started chasing Prinz, and he led them further down the mountain. After a while the soldiers became exhausted, gave up their chase, sat on a rock, and passed some schnapps back and forth. Prinz doubled back to where the others were hiding.

"What a smart dog. I will never question his guidance again," uttered Misha.

CHAPTER 20

Somewhere in the United States
Current day

"What about the commandant, Grandpa?" inquires the grandson.

"Well, he is still at Herr Strup's cabin. The soldiers are about to climb the mountain to find the dog, and the commandant is getting anxious. He knows the Jews can't be far away."

"We are climbing the mountain at dawn. Make ready to leave and … burn the cabin!" the commandant ordered.

"What about the old man?" asked a soldier.

"Burn him with the cabin," the commandant coldly replied.

"Burn him," cries the grandson. "I don't want him to die."

"He is already dead. Are you sure you want me to continue the story? Perhaps I should wait until you are little older," the grandfather ponders.

"It's okay," he says, wiping a tear from his eye. "Prinz will be all right, won't he?"

"Now don't get ahead of the story," the grandfather responds.

At dawn, the soldiers burned the cabin, gathered their belongings, and started the tough climb.

Meanwhile Prinz led Herschel and the others to the top of the first ridge of a bare, icy mountain.

"I am afraid the weather is turning colder. There could be a storm forming," warned Herschel.

"Just what we need, a snowstorm," replied Misha.

"That is not such a bad thing, Misha. The new snow will cover our tracks."

"And to think I thought *Job* had it bad. I don't want to be the next *Job*!" exclaimed Misha.

"*He* is testing us," Goldie replied.

"So *he* is, Goldie," Misha responded.

They continued to climb. The wind picked up, and snow began to blow. Prinz found cover by some large rocks, and the others followed. The blowing snow blocked the sunlight, and they struggled to see where they were. When the blizzard let up, they beheld a sight hollowed out of the surrounding rocky walls of granite.

"What have we here? Looks like the entrance to a cave!" exclaimed Herschel.

He made his way over in the blowing snow, cleared some brush, and peered inside.

"Misha, help me clear the rest of the brush."

They carefully moved some more snow and brush, totally exposing the cave entrance. Goldie, carrying Sarah, rushed to the entrance, and Prinz proceeded to enter the cave, disappearing into the dark. Herschel followed Prinz, motioning to the others to hold back until it was safe. He spotted some broken pottery and burned wood. It appeared safe enough. When Prinz returned, Herschel waved his arms to get their attention.

"Come in, and we will stay here to wait out the storm. For now we will make this our camp. There is enough wood to make a fire, and with the wind blowing in every direction, the smoke will be so diluted that it will be hard to trace," replied Herschel.

Herschel gathered the burned wood and placed it in a pile. He drew a circle in the dirt around the wood so the fire was contained. He then lit the wood with the lighter that Misha brought and fanned the flame. Schnapps and beef sticks, crackers and cheese were passed among them. They ate quietly, gazing out the cave's entrance, struggling to see through the white haze for any movement in the snow. The storm picked up intensity, and they huddled around the fire for warmth. After eating they took out the sleeping bags from the backpacks and wrapped themselves as much as they could to contain the warmth and shut out the ever-increasing cold. Prinz was in the corner of the cave chewing on a bone he had found and brought back. They were slowly drawn to sleep by the sound of the howling wind. Herschel, embracing Sophia and caressing her face, assured her that they would be safe.

Sophia, once again thinking of the baby, kissed him and said, "We need to appreciate every moment we have and treat it like our last."

They kissed once more and fell asleep in each other's arms.

CHAPTER 21

At the Cave
November 24, 1938

The morning sun seeped though the entrance of the cave. The wind had calmed considerably, and the snow had dwindled to a light dusting. Herschel rubbed his eyes and looked at the others sleeping. He rose and walked toward the back of the cave, looking for Prinz. Prinz was nowhere to be found. He called for Prinz, but there was no response.

"Wake up! Prinz is gone," exclaimed Herschel.

"Gone. But where?" asked Sophia

"Who will guide us the rest of the way if he doesn't come back?" questioned Misha.

"He is a good dog. He won't leave us, right, Nana?" Sarah asked.

"Of course not, darling. He loves you. He will be back," replied Goldie.

"I am just going to have a look outside the cave. You stay here," said Herschel. "Everything will be fine."

"Herschel, call him and maybe he will come. We will gather everything and be ready to go when you find him," Sophia said.

"I can't yell his name. What if there are soldiers nearby. Remember yesterday! I will look for him," replied Herschel.

Herschel took a couple of beef sticks to eat and a drink of the schnapps. He moved toward the front of the cave, first making his way against the side of the cave until he got to the opening. He peered out but did not see Prinz. There were animal tracks in the new snow, and he decided to follow the tracks. He thought to himself, *Could these be Prinz's tracks?* No matter—it was the only clue he had to find Prinz.

"Goldie, break out the beef sticks and bread. Sarah, you help me roll up the blankets," said Sophia. "We will be ready to go when Herschel returns with Prinz."

They rolled up the blankets, put them aside, and sat down to eat the beef sticks and some cheese and bread.

"I am tired of the beef sticks, Nana. Isn't there something else I can eat?" inquired Sarah.

"No, honey, except for the crackers. Have some cheese and crackers and a drink of your water," replied Goldie.

Sarah took the cheese and crackers and ate them. She drank the water and smiled.

"Tell you the truth, I am getting tired of the beef sticks too. We all are, but this is all we have," replied Goldie.

They anxiously waited for Herschel's return in the back of the cave. An hour passed.

"Where is he? Do you think Misha should go looking for him?" asked Goldie.

"No. Herschel said we should remain here together, and that is what we are going to do," Sophia responded.

Misha looked at the wall of the cave and pointed to a drawing he had found.

"Look at this. It looks like the Star of David. See the six points. And it looks like it is on a shield. Do you think one of the lost tribes camped here!" Misha exclaimed excitedly.

He picked up Sarah to show it to her, and she followed the outline with her finger.

"Don't be silly, Misha. This is Germany, not the Holy Land," replied Goldie.

"Quiet," whispered Sophia. "Don't forget there are still soldiers out there."

Misha examined the rest of the cave for drawings, but none were found.

Meanwhile Herschel looked for Prinz, and as he walked, he covered his tracks with a branch he was carrying. He heard laughter and ducked into some foliage and dropped to the ground. He saw two soldiers sitting on a rock, passing a flask back and forth. One soldier lit a cigarette and started speaking to the other. The other soldier laughed out loud. Herschel looked away and saw Prinz, crouched in the snow, watching and waiting. Prinz was carrying something in his mouth. After a short while, the soldiers stood and stretched, retrieved their rifles, and started down the mountain. Prinz bolted from where he was hiding and brought Herschel a rabbit he had found.

"Good boy." He patted him on the head. "Now take us back to the cave."

Prinz wagged his tail, and they set out for the cave, Herschel covering their tracks as they went.

"Did you hear that?" Sophia excitedly asked.

"Hear what, Sophia?" replied Goldie.

"A muffled sound. Like laughter, but it seems far off. Maybe Herschel found Prinz and they are coming."

"Let's greet them," said Misha.

"Can I come with you, Grandpa?" asked Sarah, running to catch up with him.

Rushing up to Misha and Sarah and grabbing them before leaving the cave, Goldie warned, "And what if it's soldiers?"

Misha realized what he had almost done, and they joined Goldie and Sophia in the back of the cave. Shadows of the two soldiers walking in the distance appeared on the cave wall. As the shadows moved across the cave opening, they crossed their faces as they crouched in the rear of the cave. Sounds of laughter and talking drifted into the distance.

"That was close. See why we should stay here. What if we had gone out like you said, Misha? What then? What if Sarah ran past you to those soldiers? This time they wouldn't miss!" exclaimed Sophia.

"You are right, Sophia. We will stay in the rear of the cave until Herschel returns," said Misha.

"And Prinz. Don't forget Prinz!" Sarah exclaimed.

It had started to snow again and was turning colder. After a short time, Herschel and Prinz entered the cave.

Rushing from the rear of the cave, Sophia said, "I am so happy to see you both." She grabbed Herschel and hugged him and in the process the rabbit he had in his hand. "What is that in your hand, Herschel?" she inquired.

"Nana, it's a rabbit. Can I have it for a pet?" pleaded Sarah.

"It wouldn't be a good pet," Goldie replied as Sarah sighed.

"What happened?" asked Sophia

"The soldiers were talking about a rabbit they shot earlier while arguing who was going to shoot Prinz. I bet this is the rabbit. Prinz found it. I think we can make a small fire and cook it. After we eat, we can start out," replied Herschel.

"Well, Sarah, looks like you are going to get something different to eat after all," responded Goldie. "I know just how to cook rabbit."

Goldie made a small fire in the rear of the cave, and Herschel stuck the rabbit on the end of a branch and held it over the fire. After a short time it was ready, and they broke off pieces to eat, throwing some to Prinz. Sarah ate but made a face.

"Wouldn't those soldiers be surprised to know we ate their rabbit?" gloated Herschel.

They finished the meal, put out the fire, and exited the cave.

All the while Misha was wondering who made the drawing in the cave and when, but there was no time to study it further, so no answer to be had. It would remain a mystery.

"Who did make the drawing, Grandpa?" asks the grandson.

"It is a mystery, at least for now," the grandfather responds.

CHAPTER 22

On the Mountain
November 24, 1938

Prinz leading the way, they slowly climbed toward the top of another ridge. The foliage was thinning, and the snow continued to fall. It was getting colder as they climbed. They came to part of the ridge that appeared to be impassable, but Prinz found a path. They tied the rope around each other with Sarah between Goldie and Misha and continued to climb using the pick and shovel.

"Be sure the rope is secure around Sarah as well," Herschel warned.

Checking the rope, Misha replied, "It is secure, Herschel."

One by one, they made their way, following Prinz. Each step was carefully approached. After climbing a few minutes, Sophia called out, "Wait. I am out of breath. Don't forget I am climbing for two."

"Two? What do you mean two? Are—are you pregnant?" Herschel yelled back.

"I wasn't going to tell you. It just slipped out. I didn't want you to worry about me and the baby too," replied Sophia.

"How long have you known?" asked Herschel.

"Remember when I saw Doctor Falik just before we left? That is when I found out. Leaving suddenly, I did not want to burden you with knowing I am pregnant," Sofia replied.

"Burden me? It is not a burden. It is joyous, even under these circumstances. I will take care of you both." He caressed her face. "Now we must keep climbing while there is light," Herschel said proudly.

CHAPTER 23

On the Mountain
November 24, 1938

Halfway to the peak Prinz paused and then lay down in the snow. Seeing Prinz, they did the same and waited. From above they heard voices, and fear gripped them. Could it be more soldiers? Had they come all this way in vain!

Herschel whispered, "We can't go on. Prinz hasn't moved. I can't tell if the voices are German."

Sophia whispered back, "Maybe they are speaking Swiss being so close to the top."

Herschel replied, "Regardless, we wait until Prinz moves."

After a short while, the voices became softer, and Prinz rose and started the upward climb once more. As they reached the top of the ridge, they realized that this was not the top of the mountain but only another obstacle they had to overcome. From the ridge they looked back toward the forest and Herr Strup's cabin. They saw the soldiers with their dogs assembling around the mountain's base. They saw the cave and realized they hadn't come that far. It was only a matter of time before the soldiers with their dogs would climb the mountain and track them.

"Is that Herr Strup's cabin?" Misha asked.

"I think so," said Herschel.

"It looks destroyed. What happened to Herr Strup?" asked Misha.

"Maybe he got away and is coming to join us," replied Herschel. "Prinz will know if that is the case."

"Grandpa. They don't know about Herr Strup, do they?"

"No," replies the grandpa.

"Who will care for Prinz?" asks the Grandson.

"You will see." The grandpa pats the grandson on the head and then the dog. "Let me see where I left off." He pauses for a moment.

It was getting dark, so they found a clearing surrounded by bushes where they could make camp. Exhausted from the day's climb, they settled down after eating the leftover rabbit and beef sticks to a good night's sleep.

Herschel, lying next to Sophia, reached out and hugged her.

"Climbing for two. Quite a feat. I am glad it slipped out. Even under these circumstances I want to know," whispered Herschel. "Our child will grow up free!"

Sophia smiled and kissed Herschel, and they fell asleep in each other's arms. The only sound heard now was a whisper of the wind and a dusting of the snow.

CHAPTER 24

At the Cave
November 25, 1938

Next morning at the cave, an old man and his daughter sought refuge from the snow and saw the remnants of a recent fire. They knew others had escaped. Perhaps they could join them, only if they knew where they were. They emerged from the cave and looked toward the ridge. They saw two people standing at the ledge looking back toward them. They immediately motioned with their arms to attract their attention.

"Over there by the cave, look, Herschel," exclaimed Misha. "There are two people waving their arms."

Herschel looked and tried to make out who they were. From his vantage point he could see they were not soldiers. He thought they must be others that escaped. He waved back to them, and they responded with another wave.

"I am going back to get them. Tell the others," said Herschel. He called over Prinz, and they descended the ridge, backtracking to the cave. Misha told the others what was happening.

Sophia, worried, said, "They could be huntsman. This could be a trick."

Misha replied, "It is an old man and a young girl. They are like us—escaping. It will be all right."

Herschel and Prinz made their way toward the old man and young girl and upon reaching them realized it was the rabbi and his daughter, Julia.

The rabbi, seeing Herschel, pointed to the sky and said a prayer.

"Rabbi. What happened? How did you get here? Do you have a guide?" asked Herschel.

"No guide, Herschel. Just kept walking after they burned the synagogue. Julia had climbed the mountain before, so she knew enough to get us this far," replied the rabbi. "This cave is as far as she had come. See, she drew the shield of David on the cave wall some time ago," he said, pointing back toward the drawing.

Pointing to the dog, Herschel said, "Prinz is our guide. He knows the mountains and how to get to Switzerland. You come with us."

"We can't stay here. I see no other way but to join you," the rabbi said, sighing.

They slowly ascended the ridge and after a while reached the others. By the time they all assembled it was getting dark, so they decided to spend another night at the top of the ridge. Tomorrow they would continue their climb. The rabbi and Julia recounted how they escaped, and after sharing stories, they ate and took out the sleeping bags. Misha was happy to hear how the drawing appeared on the wall of the cave. His mystery had been solved.

CHAPTER 25

At the Cave
November 25, 1938

German soldiers approached the cave after having climbed from the cabin.

"Search over there," the commandant ordered, pointing to the opening of the cave.

"Over here, Commandant. Looks like a fire was made," a soldier said, pointing to the rear of the cave.

"And look at this drawing. Only *Jews* would make such a picture."

The commandant went to the rear of the cave and felt the burnt embers. Still warm. He looked at the drawing.

"They were here all right. Tell the others to make camp. They can't be far ahead," yelled the commandant. "Tomorrow we will surprise them. Now hurry, before it is too dark."

Two soldiers from the previous day arrived at the cave and were escorted to the commandant.

"Herr Commandant, these soldiers say they spotted a dog on the mountain a couple days ago."

"Could be Herr Strups's dog," pondered the commandant. "Where did you see him?"

"Not far from here. I was going to shoot the dog," the soldier replied.

"You didn't shoot it? Because if you did, I would be very unhappy. That dog will lead us to the Jews that Herr Strup was helping to escape," shouted the commandant.

"That is what I was thinking, Herr Commandant. I did not shoot it," the soldier meekly replied.

CHAPTER 26

On the Mountain
November 26, 1938

The next day with the weather turning colder and the snow starting to fall once again, Prinz was leading them up another ridge, everyone secured by the rope. The footing was slick, and they had to climb slowly and steadily. Carefully inserting the hooks that Herr Strup gave them using the ice pick and securing the rope, they climbed one by one.

"How far is the camp, Herschel?" asked Misha.

"According to the map, the camp is just over the top of the mountain. Part of the mountain is in Germany, and the rest is in Switzerland. By tomorrow, we should be close enough to see the camp," assured Herschel.

"Will someone come from the camp to greet us?" asked Misha

"I don't know. Prinz knows the way, so we might be on our own. No matter though, we have come this far, so we can certainly find the camp," Herschel responded.

"We are making very good progress. Prinz certainly knows the best route!" exclaimed Sophia.

Meanwhile at the base of the first ridge, the soldiers were commencing their climb.

"Keep up! We must catch up to them before they cross into Switzerland. Hurry, they must not get away!" yelled the commandant.

The soldiers reached the top and crossed over, following the same route that Prinz took. They stopped to examine tracks in the snow.

"There are seven of them—see the tracks," said a soldier, pointing to the snow. "One is a child."

"Over here," yelled another soldier. "These are dog tracks. Probably the same dog we saw on the mountain a couple of days ago."

"Now we know we have the same *Jews* that were at the cabin. Obviously the dog is helping them cross. If we follow the tracks, it should lead us right to them!" exclaimed the commandant.

Meanwhile at the top of the ridge, Herschel paused and looked back, seeing fresh meadows in the distance. Misha struggled to keep up.

"Herschel, I need to stop, catch my breath," said Misha, while carrying Sarah up the ridge.

"Prinz," called out Herschel. Prinz stopped in his tracks and knelt.

"How much longer, Herschel? My legs are freezing!" exclaimed Goldie.

"So are mine," he replied.

Sophia took out the thermos, and they passed it among themselves, each taking a drink of the schnapps to keep them warm. Sarah drank her water. Prinz swallowed some snow and chewed on a blade of grass he found peeking through the snow. After a short while, they climbed some more, unaware of the approaching soldiers. Before they reached the top of the second ridge, it was dusk. They hurried so as to climb while there was still light. They reached the top of the second ridge just as dark descended, and the light of the moon glistening off the snow revealed a clearing for their campsite. They spread out the sleeping bags and shared the food and schnapps.

Before they settled down to sleep, the rabbi offered a prayer.

"May the Lord protect us and keeps us from the soldiers. May the Lord shine his light upon us and be our guide to the camp. Amen."

Meanwhile, after climbing the first ridge, the soldiers decided to make camp since it was too dark to continue, even though the commandant wanted to keep going. For the soldiers' morale, he agreed to make camp in a small clearing. Tomorrow, he conjectured, was the day of reckoning for those Jews.

CHAPTER 27

On the Mountain
November 26, 1938

The following day they came to a steep ridge, and seeing the solders gaining on them, Herschel called Prinz over and removed some of the diamonds he had been carrying. He spread the stones on the top of the ridge to be visible to the soldiers when they approached the ridge, hoping to distract them and slow them down. Prinz took them down a steep ice slope. Once again they tied the rope to each other and fastened it to the ice axe jammed behind a large rock. Misha carried Sarah. They went down one by one, Herschel and Misha leading the way, Prinz already having descended on his own.

Goldie followed. "My ankle feels like it's about to give way, Misha," yelled Goldie.

Misha passed Sarah to Herschel and partially ascended the slope to assist Goldie. Once Goldie had descended, Sophia and Julia followed. The rabbi, insisting on being the last to descend, held back.

Sophia carefully descended and ended up in the arms of Herschel.

Julia, being an experienced climber, followed without a problem, leaving the rabbi to bring up the rear.

"Come on, Rabbi," yelled Herschel. "Go down backward. Put one foot behind the other and slowly descend. You have the rope to catch you if you fall."

Encouraged by his daughter, the rabbi, weary of the descent, said a prayer and started down, first one foot then the other. Just before he got halfway down, there was a loud roar. A huge bear looked over the ridge and snapped at him, pulling on the rope. The rabbi panicked as the rope snapped. He lost his foothold on the side of the ice slope and fell to the bottom. They rushed to the rabbi, but it was too late. His head hit a sharp rock, and the damage was too great even for Herschel to save him.

After pausing and reflecting on just what happened, they found some soft ground in which to dig at the base of the slope, and saying some prayers, they buried the rabbi. Julia fashioned a Star of David out of some sticks she found and placed it at the head of the grave. Herschel comforted her, and the rest of the party moved away to give Julia some quiet time with her father. After a short while, Herschel said it was time to move on and called Prinz over to lead them away from the base of the slope. Reluctantly they followed Prinz across a level area to a frozen creek bed with just enough flowing water to allow them to drink. There they paused to drink and eat and catch their breath, all along thinking about the rabbi.

"Did the rabbi have to die, Grandpa?" inquires the grandson.

Consoling the grandson, he replies, "No, he did not have to die. It is just what happened. Now where was I ..."

At the first ridge the commandant ordered his men to hasten their pace and when approaching the second ridge, to climb without caution so as to catch up to the Jews. He pressed the soldiers to point of exhaustion and fearing a rebellion, gave in and allowed them to rest.

At the frozen creek Herschel implored them to keep moving and now not only be on the lookout for the soldiers but for any wildlife as well. As they crossed the little valley, fog set in and it became harder and harder to see. They followed Prinz to other side of the valley and reached another ridge to climb. Fortunately when the rope broke, it fell back toward them. Otherwise there would have been no way to safely join them together for another climb.

At the second ridge the lead soldiers approached and spotted the diamonds that Herschel had dispersed. They threw down their rifles and began gathering the stones. Others did likewise, causing confusion and delay. The commandant, seeing what was happening, fired his sidearm in the air and ordered them to pick up their weapons and descend the ridge. He went over to a lookout to see if he could spot the Jews at the base of the ridge. One of the soldiers ventured to the edge of the slope and saw tracks in the snow and alerted the commandant.

"There are prints in the snow by the edge of the slope," said the soldier. "And here behind this boulder is part of a rope tied to an ice axe. They obviously descended here."

The commandant rushed over and looked. He called the rest of the soldiers over, and they prepared to follow the trail left behind. The commandant tried to see where in the valley below the Jews might have gone but because of the dense fog saw nothing. They fastened a rope to the ice axe and slowly descended the slope one by one, the commandant going first.

From out of nowhere came the bear, charging the soldiers gathered at the slope awaiting their turn. The bear grabbed one of the soldiers from behind as he fired his rifle to distract him, but it was too late. The bear drug the soldier in the snow and ran off, and the remaining soldiers, in a panic, descended hastily.

Herschel, hearing the rifle shot, knew the soldiers were not far behind. For now the heavy fog would hide them, but when it lifted, they would be exposed.

At the base of the slope the soldiers found the rabbi's grave and knew they had one less Jew to capture. The fog was so thick now that the commandant ordered the soldiers to make camp.

"When the fog lifts in the morning, we shall overtake them. They can't be far."

Meanwhile Prinz found a small crevasse protected by a cluster of bushes. Herschel decided with dusk on the horizon and the fog thickening in the valley, it would be safer to make camp there.

Julia, distraught over the loss of her father and fearful of the soldiers, disagreed.

"We must keep moving," she cried. "The Germans won't rest until they capture all of us. We owe it to my father to survive!"

Herschel, understanding her concern, went over and comforted her. The others joined in. He reassured her that the first thing in the morning they would go. After they ate and made ready the sleeping bags, Herschel decided they should have a service to remember the rabbi. He gathered them in a circle and led them in prayer. As Julia wept, they said their final good-byes to the rabbi, vowing someday to return and properly bury him in a Jewish cemetery.

CHAPTER 28

Rachel Stern's Camp in Switzerland
November 26, 1938

Just across from the next ridge was a ski lodge converted into a refugee camp. Tents were set up to accommodate the refugees, and the lodge converted to offices and a dining hall. A watchtower had been placed at the top of the ski lift, manned by armed guards. This was Rachel Stern's camp. Refugees assembled in a common area for news about what was happening in Germany.

Rachel motioned to an associate at the gathering, and they went outside the lodge.

"He should have been here by now, Hymie. After all, Herr Strup's dog knows the way to the camp. When I spoke to Herr Strup several days ago, he told me when Herschel would be leaving the cabin."

A runner came up with a note for her and handed it to her. As she read, she looked shaken.

"Our source says that Herr Strup was killed by the soldiers and his cabin burned. That means the Germans know about Herschel. Hymie, go with Isaac up the mountain. Find him before the soldiers do!"

"Isaac, get the rifles and some provisions. We're going up the mountain to find him!" exclaimed Hymie.

"I will contact the Swiss Border soldiers and let them know you are looking for Herschel and warn them that the Germans may not be far behind," assured Rachel.

Isaac and Hymie said their good-byes and slowly ascended the mountain.

"Do they find Herschel?" asks the grandson.

"Wait and see," replies the grandpa, patting the dog and stretching. After he sits, he continues.

CHAPTER 29

On the Mountain
November 27, 1938

The following morning, the fog still thick, the soldiers crossed the valley toward the frozen creek. The commandant urged them to pick up the pace. Herschel woke the others before dawn, and they followed Prinz through the crevasse and up another ridge, hoping this was the last crossing before arriving at the refugee camp. Prinz was several paces ahead of Herschel, who was assisting Sophia over the very unsteady terrain. Goldie and Julia followed. At the rear was Misha, carrying Sarah.

"Slow down," yelled Misha. He stepped into a narrow opening in the ice and twisted his ankle, falling down with Sarah. Herschel, seeing this, called to Prinz to stop, and he doubled back to help Misha. Sarah had suffered a small cut on her leg but otherwise was fine. Misha, however, could hardly walk on the twisted ankle.

"I need to secure your ankle, Misha. Wait here," ordered Herschel. He took Sarah to the others and contemplated what he could wrap around the ankle. He asked the others what they might have that they could spare to use as a brace for Misha's ankle.

Goldie replied, "How about the elastic in my stockings?" She took her stockings off and handed them to Herschel.

He wrapped the stockings around Misha's ankle as tight as he could and then wedged his foot into his shoe with a small stick he had found.

"See if you can put your weight on your ankle," Herschel said.

Misha stood up and carefully put his leg down. The ankle hurt, but he could stand on it. He then slowly walked toward Herschel.

"It will have to do," said Misha. "Just take it slow, please."

"That was a neat way to fix Misha's ankle," exclaims the grandson. "Maybe I should carry one of my mother's stockings with me just in case I hurt my ankle."

The grandpa smiles and continues.

The climb this time was not as steep but because of Misha's injury took longer.

The soldiers crossed the valley, found the frozen river, and then made their way toward the ridge. The fog was lifting, and in a distance they could see Herschel and the others following Prinz up the ridge. Excited, the commandant ordered them to pick up the pace. Soon they would be in range of their rifles.

At the top of the ridge, Herschel looked toward the direction Prinz was pointing and in the distance could see the camp. He told the others, and they all stared at the camp.

"How far do you think it is?" inquired Misha.

"I wish Prinz could tell us. It could be close, or that might be an illusion and we still have a way to go," replied Herschel.

Prinz, knowing the direction of the camp, led them over a small rise and then started a descent. It was slow going with Misha's hurt ankle. At one point Herschel had to steady Misha while Goldie struggled to assist Sarah. Sophia, stressed by the pace, wanted to rest but knew they must keep going. The further they descend, the closer the camp appeared.

CHAPTER 30

On the Mountain
November 27, 1938

The soldiers reached the bottom of the ridge and prepared to climb. As the first soldier was hoisted up, another bear charged, grabbing the soldier and becoming twisted in the rope. The more the bear struggled to free itself from the rope, the more it became entangled. The commandant took his sidearm and shot the bear, freeing the soldier along with the rope. Stepping over the bear, he ordered the soldiers to commence the climb once more. Herschel, hearing another gunshot, yelled to hurry because the soldiers were not far behind.

"How are we going to defend ourselves?" asked Misha.

"The best defense is to keep going, no matter what," replied Herschel.

"I have an idea. You go ahead with the rest. Follow Prinz. I will stay back to distract the soldiers."

Sophia objected. "If you are staying back, so am I. Two is a better distraction than one."

Herschel replied, "No. You are carrying our baby. You must go for the baby's sake. I will be careful."

Reluctantly they followed Prinz over a small rise and disappeared.

Herschel covered their tracks and made fresh tracks in the opposite direction to throw off the soldiers. After he was finished, he walked back, covering his tracks as he went, and took refuge behind some snow-covered rocks.

Prinz led the rest down the slope and entered the refugee camp. Rachel Stern rushed over to greet them and asked for Herschel. Sophia explained that Herschel held back to divert the soldiers to allow them time to escape to the camp.

Rachel told them that two of her men had been dispatched to assist Herschel, and they should not worry; the Germans can't cross into Switzerland. She also told them the Swiss Mountain soldiers had been notified and they would make sure Herschel was safe. She told them to join the other refugees, drink, and have a real meal and then to return to her. By then Herschel should be at the camp.

Prinz, seeing that Sophia and the others were settled, secretly retreated from the camp and climbed the mountain in search of Herschel.

CHAPTER 31

On the Mountain
November 27, 1938

"Herr Commandant. Over here. New tracks," yelled one of the soldiers.

They all rushed over.

"See, the dog is leading them. Follow those tracks," yelled the commandant.

They followed the tracks for a short while, but they led away from the refugee camp. The commandant realized the trick and ordered the soldiers to go back and shoot anything that moved. Herschel, seeing the soldiers, took the bait, rose, and started running toward a small rise. One of the soldiers saw him and fired his rifle, hitting Herschel in the leg.

"I shot one of them, Commandant," yelled a soldier. As the rest of the soldiers rushed toward Herschel, Prinz sprung out of nowhere and began dragging Herschel over the rise. At the same time, Hymie and Isaac, rifles drawn, rushed to them, firing as they went.

The German soldiers took cover and commenced firing back.

"Are you from the camp?" Herschel asked.

Isaac replied, "Yes. You are wounded. I will help you the rest of the way. The soldiers can't cross over this side. We are in Switzerland."

Hymie maintained his position and fired another round in the direction of the soldiers, allowing Isaac, Herschel, and Prinz to proceed toward the camp.

The commandant ordered the soldiers to rush Hymie's position when Swiss soldiers appeared and turned the Germans away. Unknowingly the German soldiers had crossed into Switzerland. Reluctantly the commandant ordered a retreat. Hymie, having joined up with the Swiss soldiers and seeing the German soldiers retreat, thanked them and returned to the camp. Herschel and Isaac had already arrived, and Herschel's leg was being attended to. After a while, Herschel, Sophia, Goldie, Sarah, and Julia joined the rest of the refugees, and they celebrated their escape. Prinz was the hero, and for his reward, he was given another big, juicy bone to chew on.

CHAPTER 32

Somewhere in the United States
Current day

"That was a great story, Grandpa," says the grandson. "What happens next? What about the baby?"

"I am going to tell you," the grandfather continues.

"They stayed at the refugee camp for several weeks, allowing Herschel's leg to heal. Herschel gave the rest of the diamonds to Rachel Stern, and she secured passports for Julia, Misha, Goldie, and Sarah to go to Israel. After a few days, they departed, saying their good-byes. Herschel and Sophia decided to come to the United States. Passports were issued and passage secured, and they left."

"What about Prinz?" asks the grandson.

"Herschel wanted to take Prinz with them, but the Swiss authorities would not allow it. After Herschel and Sophia settled in the United States and Sophia had her baby, they finally secured passage for Prinz, who had been living with Rachel Stern, and he joined them at their home in America," replies the grandpa.

"Where do they live, Grandpa?"

"Not far from us," he responds. "Now time for bed." He hugs the Grandson and carries him to his room, the old dog following.

After retreating to the den, he hugs his dog and says, "One day I will tell him your *real* name."

CPSIA information can be obtained
at www.ICGtesting.com
Printed in the USA
FFOW05n2337100217